Ignaz Pleyel

Three Quartetts, Dedicated to His Majesty the King of

Prussia

Ignaz Pleyel

Three Quartetts, Dedicated to His Majesty the King of Prussia

ISBN/EAN: 9783337298234

Printed in Europe, USA, Canada, Australia, Japan

Cover: Foto ©Andreas Hilbeck / pixelio.de

More available books at **www.hansebooks.com**

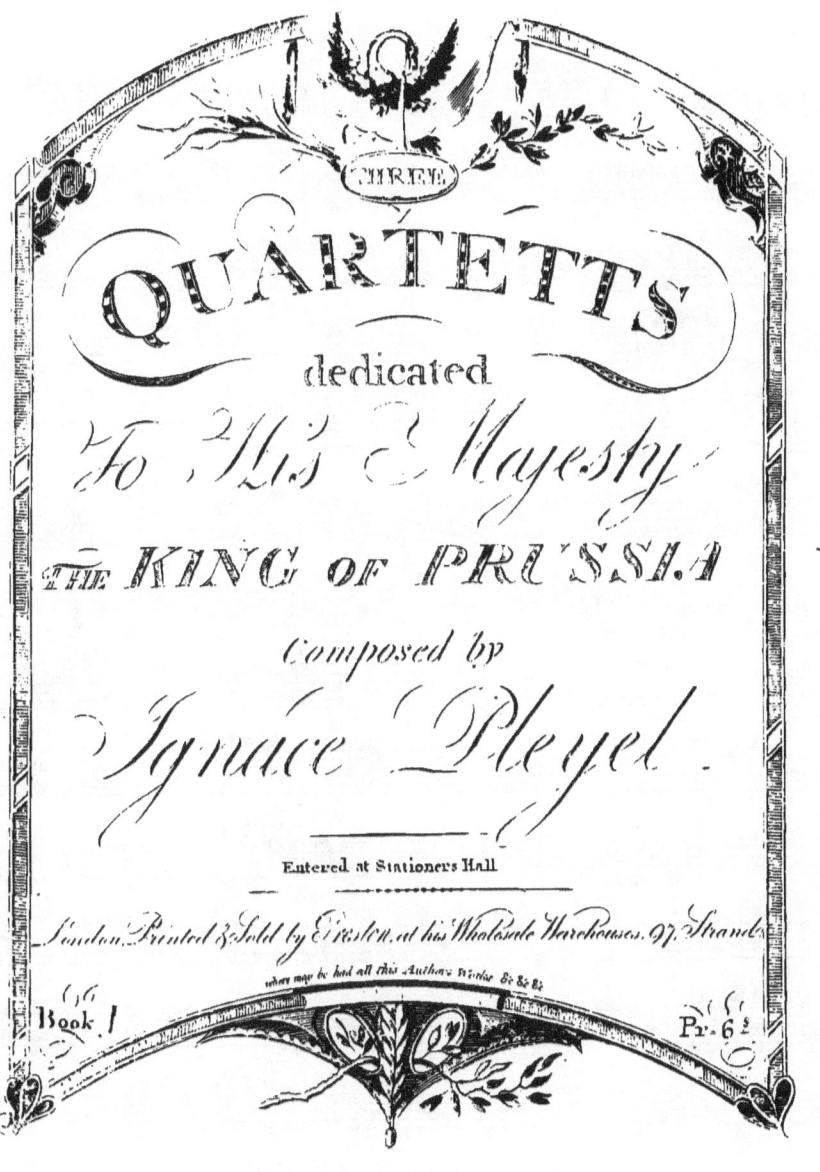

THREE

QUARTETTS

dedicated

To His Majesty

THE *KING* OF *PRUSSIA*

Composed by

Ignace Pleyel

Entered at Stationers Hall

London, Printed & Sold by Preston, at his Wholesale Warehouses, 97, Strand

where may be had all this Authors Works &c &c &c

Book 1

Pr. 6 ͬ

QUARTETTO 1

Moderato

Pleyel's Quartets (K of P) Nº 1

Pleyel's Quartets (K. of P.) No. I

QUARTETTO II

Pleyel's Quartets (K. of P.) Nº 1

Adagio
Espressivo

Rondo

Pleyels Quartetts (K of P) Nᵒ 1

QUARTETTO III

Allegro agitato

Pleyels Quartetts (Kof B) N⁰ 1

Adagio
non troppo

Rondo
Allegretto

Pleyels Quartetts (K of P) Nº 1.

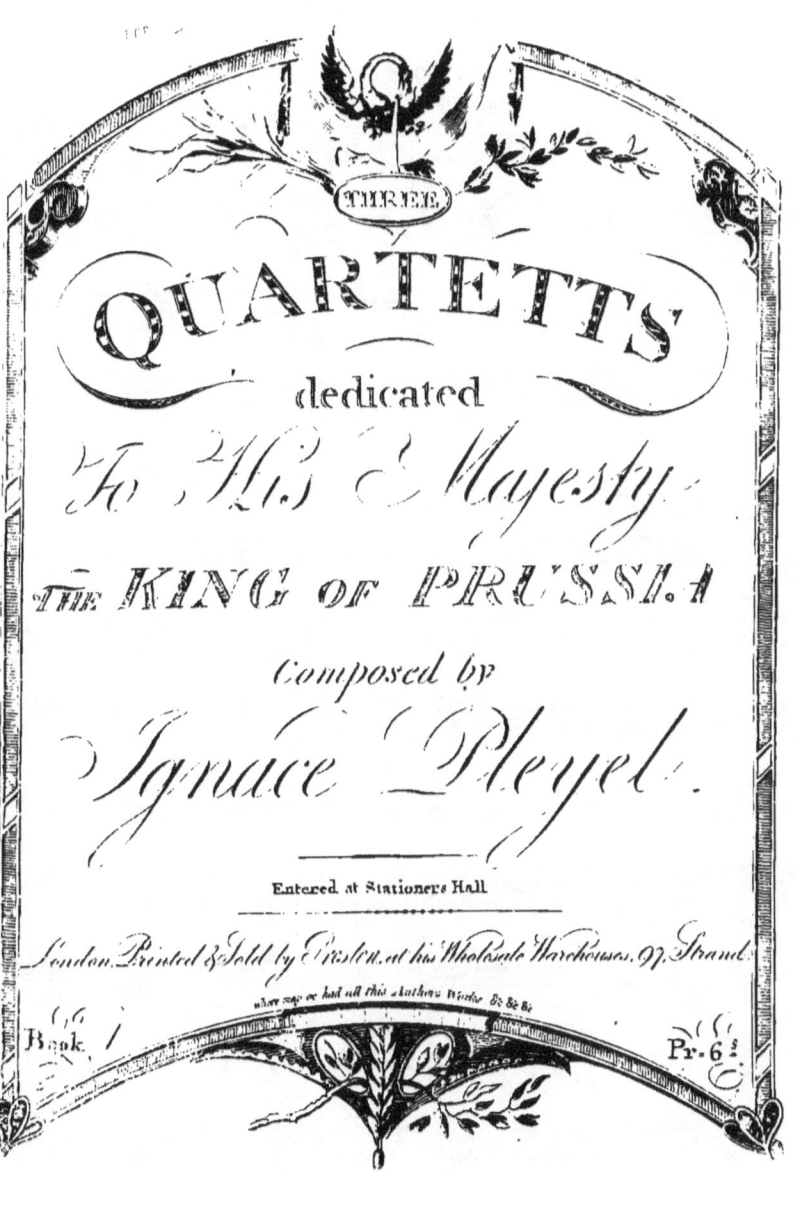

THREE

QUARTETTS

dedicated

To His Majesty

THE KING OF PRUSSIA

Composed by

Ignace Pleyel

Entered at Stationers Hall

London, Printed & Sold by Preston, at his Wholesale Warehouses, 97 Strand

where may be had all this Authors Works &c &c &c

Book 1   Pr. 6.ᵉ

2

VIOLINO SECONDO $\mathcal{N}$ 33062

Moderato

QUARTETTO I

Pleyel's Quartetts (K of P) N° 1

Pleyel's Quartetts (K of P) No. 1

S'attaca Subito

Pleyels Quartetts (K of P) N.º 1

Pleyel's Quartetts (K of P) Nº 1

QUARTETTO II

Pleyel's Quartetts (K.of P.) N°. 1.

Pleyels Quartetts (K of P) Nº 1

Pleyels Quartetts (K of P) Nº 1

QUARTETTO III

Allegro agitato

Pleyels Quartetts (K of P) Nº 1

Pleyels Quartetts (K of P) Nº 1

Pleyels Quartetts (K of P) No 1

Pleyels Quartetts (K of P) Nº 1.

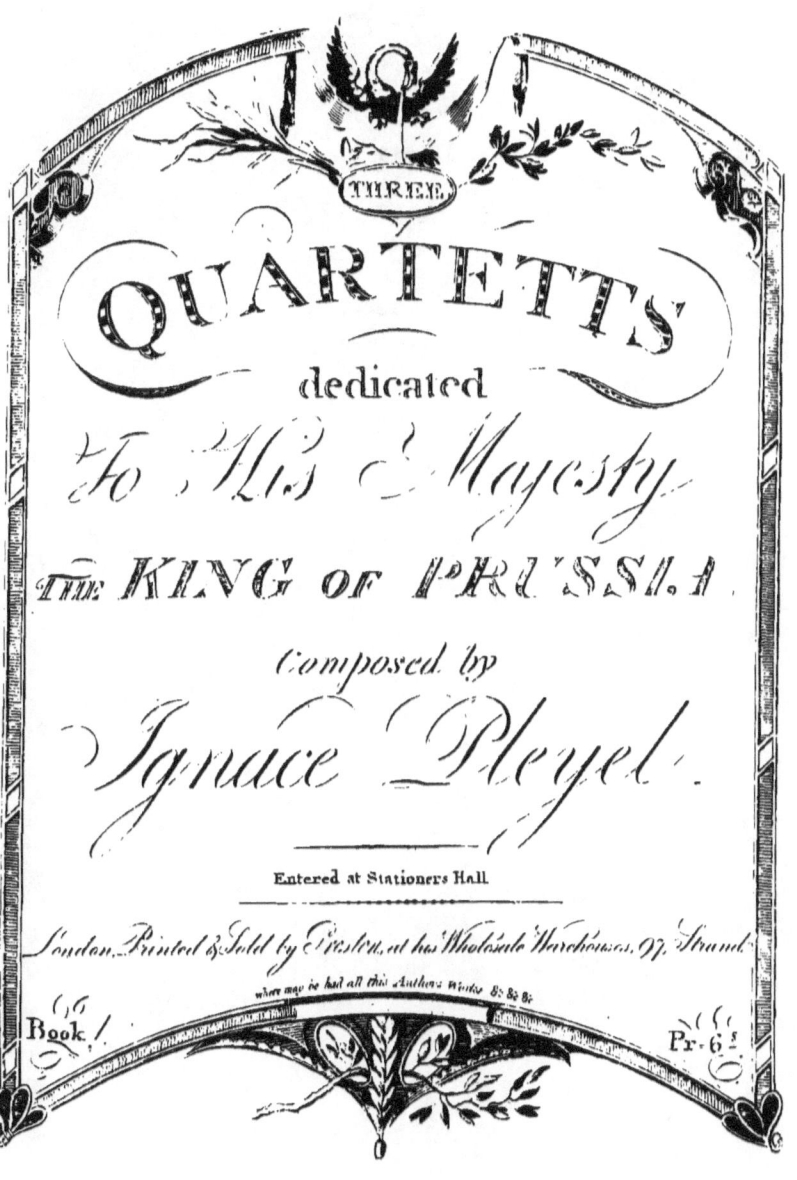

QUARTTETO I. Moderato

2

VIOLA

Pleyels Quartetts (K of P) Nº 1

4

QUARTETTO

Pleyel's Quartetts (K of P) Nº 1

Pleyels Quartetts(K of P)Nº 1

Adagio
Espressivo

Rondeau

Pleyels Quartetts K of P Nº 1

Pleyeles Quartetts (K of P) N⁰1 ƒ

ALTO

Allegro agitato

QUARTETTO III

Pleyels Quartetts K of P N.º 1

Pleyels Quartetts (K of P)Nᵒ 1

Pleyels Quartetts K of P N°1

Pleyels Quartetts (K of P) N.º 1.

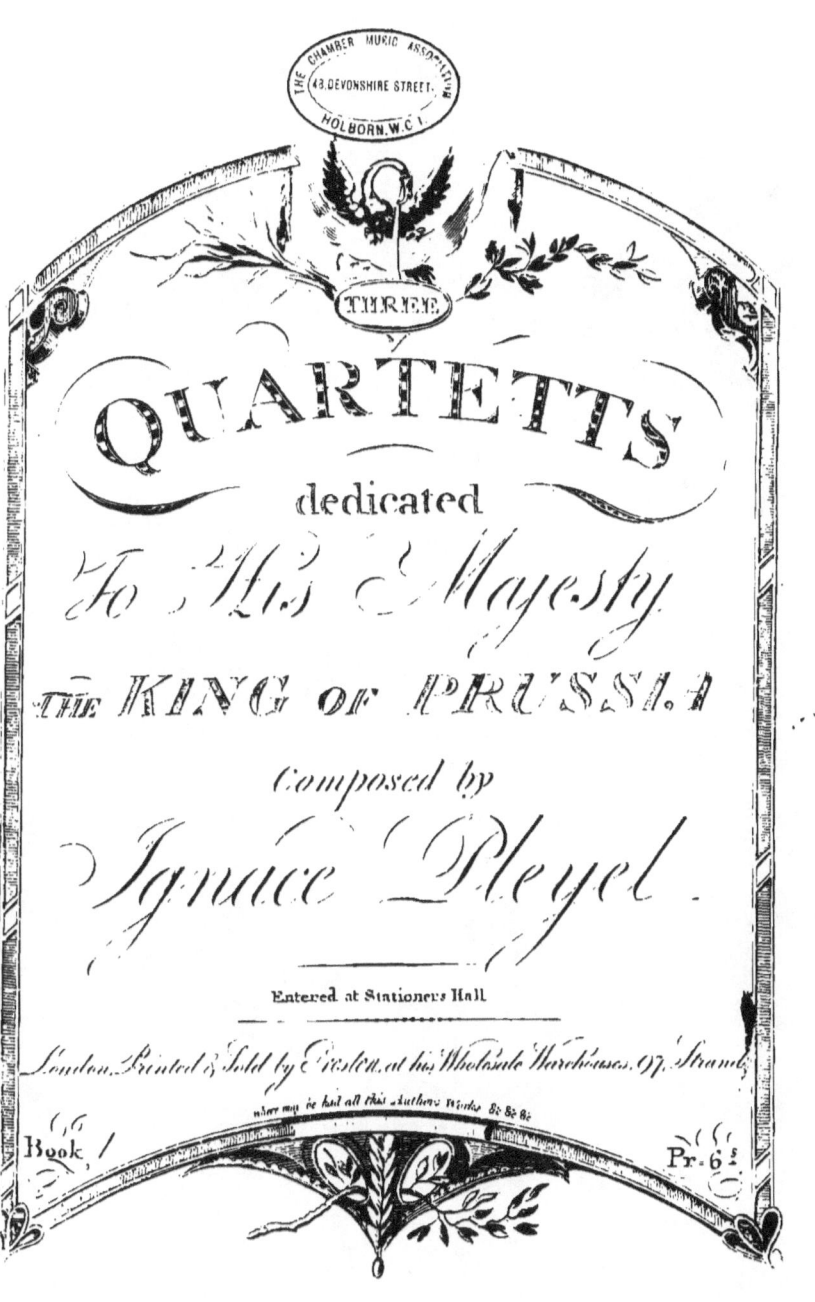

THREE

QUARTETTS

dedicated

To His Majesty

THE KING OF PRUSSIA

Composed by

Ignace Pleyel.

Entered at Stationers Hall

London, Printed & Sold by Preston, at his Wholesale Warehouses, 97, Strand.

where may be had all this Authors Works &c &c &c

Book 1

Pr. 6 s

QUARTETTO **I**

Moderato

Pleyel's Quartetts (K of P) Nº 1.

Pleyels Quartetts (Kof P) No. 1.

QUARTETTO **II**

Pleyels Quartetts (K of P) No 1

Adagio
Espressivo

Rondeau

Pleyels Quartetts (K of P) N.º 1

QUARTETTO III

Allegro Agitato

Pleyel's Quartets (K. of P.) N.º 1.

Pleyel's Quartets (K. of P.) No. 1.

10   BASSO

Adagio
non troppo

Rondeau
Allegretto

Pleyel's Quartets Krbf P. Nº 1.

Pleyel's Quartets (K. of P.) N.º 1.

www.ingramcontent.com/pod-product-compliance
Lightning Source LLC
Chambersburg PA
CBHW030854260626
47169CB00008B/2538